Hi! I'm Darcy J. Doyle, Daring Detective,

but you can call me D. J. The only thing I like better than reading a good mystery is solving one. When Brittany Bar_____'s fancy poodle disappeared just before _____ had to do something a_____ about The Case of the _____

Other books in the Darcy J. Doyle, Daring Detective series:

The Case of the Choosey Cheater
The Case of the Giggling Ghost
The Case of the Mixed-Up Monsters

Darcy J. Doyle
Daring Detective

The Case of the
Pampered Poodle

Linda Lee Maifair

ZondervanPublishingHouse
Grand Rapids, Michigan

A Division of HarperCollinsPublishers

The Case of the Pampered Poodle
Copyright © 1993 by Linda Lee Maifair

Requests for information should be addressed to:
Zondervan Publishing House
Grand Rapids, Michigan 49530

Library of Congress Cataloging-in-Publication Data

Maifair, Linda Lee.
　　The case of the pampered poodle / Linda Lee Maifair.
　　　　p. cm. — (Darcy J. Doyle, Daring Detective)
　　Summary: When her snobby classmate Brittany loses her
expensive poodle on the day of the pet show, Darcy Doyle agrees
to find the missing dog.
　　ISBN 0-310-57891-4
　　[1. Dogs—Fiction. 2. Lost and found possessions—Fiction.
3. Mystery and detective stories.] I. Title. II. Series: Maifair,
Linda Lee. Darcy J. Doyle, Daring Detective.
PZ7.M2776Cav　1993
[Fic]—dc20　　　　　　　　　　　　　　　　92-39016
　　　　　　　　　　　　　　　　　　　　　　　CIP
　　　　　　　　　　　　　　　　　　　　　　　AC

Edited by Lori J. Walburg
Interior design by Rachel Hostetter
Illustrations by Tim Davis

Printed in the United States of America

95 96 97 / ❖ LP / 10 9 8 7 6 5 4

For my father,
with love and gratitude.
Like Darcy's dad,
he has always been there
when I needed him;
he has encouraged me to do my best.

CHAPTER 1

I'm Darcy J. Doyle. Some of my friends call me Darcy. Some just call me D.J. If I keep on solving important cases, pretty soon everyone will be calling me Darcy J. Doyle, Daring Detective. It's only a matter of time.

My last big case started when we did pet reports in Miss Woodson's language arts class.

"My faithful bloodhound looks for clues and helps me solve important cases," I told the class. "He's always ready to protect me. He's the smartest, bravest dog in the world." I showed them a picture of Max.

"That's no bloodhound," Sammy Lee said. "That's just a—"

I gave him one of my looks. "Max is a master of disguise," I told him. The rest of the kids thought it was funny.

"Class!" Miss Woodson is even better at giving looks than I am. The giggling and snickering stopped. "Go on, Darcy."

I wrapped up my report. "I couldn't have solved The Case of the Giggling Ghost or the Case of the Mixed-Up Monsters without good old Max."

Brittany Barthwell wrinkled up her nose. It was something she was good at. "My Fifi has three honor certificates from the Carlton Canine Academy," she said.

Brittany had already told us about her fancy miniature poodle and her obedience school diplomas when she did her own pet report. She'd also told us all about Fifi's champion bloodline,

her shelf full of ribbons and trophies, and her designer-made food and water bowls. I was pretty tired of hearing about Fifi, but I didn't say so. I couldn't. Brittany Barthwell was my Special Project for April.

It was my Sunday school teacher, Mrs. Benson's, idea. "Think of someone you don't like very much," she'd told us. "Treat them the way you'd want to be treated, the way you'd treat a friend. You might be surprised how it turns out."

Deciding on Brittany Barthwell was easy. Nobody liked Brittany very much. She was always bragging about what she had and what she did and how much better her family was than everybody else's. I'd been trying for three days to treat her the way I wanted to be treated, like a friend. So far, I hadn't been very surprised.

She wrinkled her nose at Max's picture as if she were looking at a pile of old sweaty socks.

"My Fifi goes to The Poodle Parlor to be shampooed and trimmed every two weeks. *She* never looks unkempt."

I wasn't sure what *unkempt* meant, but I didn't like the way Brittany said it. I reminded myself to look it up in a dictionary the first chance I got. I also had to remind myself that Brittany Barthwell was my Special Project. Otherwise, I might have bopped her.

I didn't tell her I thought Fifi was a pretty dumb name for a dog. I smiled, hoping my clenched teeth didn't show. "I'd like to see your dog sometime, Brittany," I said.

Brittany gave me a funny, surprised sort of look. "I showed you a picture. Yesterday, when I did my report."

She had. A picture of a small white dog with a funny haircut, pink polish on its toenails, and matching pink ribbons on its ears and tail. I'd take good old Max anytime. "I mean the *real* Fifi," I said.

"What a wonderful idea, Darcy!" Miss Woodson beamed at me. "We could have a pet show! Then we could see all the pets you've been writing about. It would be a wonderful way to finish our unit."

Everybody but Brittany thought it would be fun. I thought she'd be glad to have a chance to show off, but she had one objection after another.

"Mother would never permit it."

"Our insurance doesn't cover such things."

"Fifi might catch a cold in this weather."

"She has a big competition to prepare for."

"I can't have poor Fifi associating with . . ." She gave Max's picture another sweaty-sock look. ". . . ordinary dogs."

I decided I would be real glad when April was over and I could go back to treating Brittany Barthwell the way she treated everybody else. Unfortunately, April had just started. I had to be nice to Brittany for another three and a half weeks if it killed me. "We couldn't have a show without Fifi," I said.

Miss Woodson agreed. "You could demonstrate the way you show her in competition, Brittany. It would be very educational!"

It turned out to be a whole lot of trouble.

CHAPTER 2

It isn't easy to wash sixty pounds of slippery, squirming fur, even when your pesty brother volunteers to help.

Allen sat on top of the wet soapy dog, trying to keep him in the bathtub long enough for me to rinse off the lather. "What did she say about Max?" he asked.

"She said he was unkempt," I told him. "It means messy." I started to hose off the suds.

Max let out a howl, cleared the rim of the tub in a leap, and bounded out of the bathroom, leaving a trail of wet paw prints all the way. "Get him!" I told Allen.

We chased Max down the hall, through the

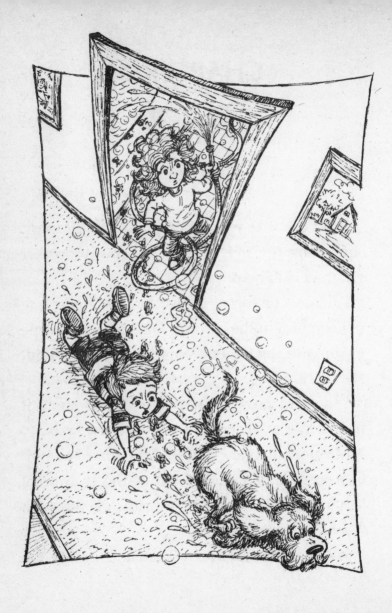

bedrooms, across Mom and Dad's bed, and down the stairs. He slid down the hallway and through the kitchen, not even bothering to slow down as he bumped open the back door and ran into the yard. He was rolling in the dirt under the swing set when we caught up to him.

The only way we could get him back into the house was by leaving a trail of chocolate chip cookies between the swing set and the door.

"Come on, Max," I begged. "You can't let Brittany Barthwell's puffy little poodle win all the prizes." I showed him another cookie. "This is important to me!"

Good old Max. No sacrifice is too great when it comes to helping me out. He followed me and the box of cookies up the stairs and into the bathroom.

This time we were smart enough to shut the door. Allen and I crawled into the tub with him, clothes and all, and turned on the shower. The shower took three minutes. It took me an hour and a half to clean up the house. But it was worth all the trouble. Washed and brushed and wearing the new blue collar Dad had bought for him, Max looked beautiful.

"He's sure to win a prize," Mom assured me the next morning as she helped me drag Max out of the station wagon in front of the school playground.

I agreed. I could hardly wait for Brittany Barthwell to see him. Special Project or not, I couldn't wait to show up her and her precious little Fifi. Max would be the bravest, smartest, handsomest pet there.

The show was scheduled to start at nine, first thing in the morning, so our parents could take the pets home afterward. By nine-fifteen Max had eaten a whole trayful of cookies off the refreshment table. Sammy's cocker spaniel had chased Mandy's calico cat up a tree, and nobody had figured out how to get it down. Nick's German shepherd had dug up half the newly sprouted daffodil bulbs the Earth Savers club had planted around the flagpole. Leon's terrier had nipped the principal on the ankle. Just about everything and everybody was howling or growling. And Brittany and Fifi still hadn't come.

Miss Woodson looked as annoyed as I felt. "Well," she said, "I guess we'll just have to start without them." She motioned for us to line up with our pets along the edge of the playground. "We'll start with a pet parade," she said.

She put on a tape of something she called "marching music" and we started walking along the inside of the fence. It was slow moving since the animals all wanted to go in different directions. We'd only gotten half way around the basketball court when Brittany came running across the playground.

Miss Woodson didn't even remind her that she was a half hour late. "Why Brittany," she said, "where's your dog?"

Brittany burst into tears. "Oh . . . Miss . . . Woodson!" she sobbed. "My Fifi . . . is gone!"

CHAPTER 3

Brittany Barthwell was on her fifth soggy tissue by the time she'd finished telling us how Fifi had disappeared in the middle of Milton Park.

"She saw a squirrel." Sob. Sniff. "And she pulled the leash right out of my hand." Sniff. Sob. "And the next thing I knew . . ." Sob. Sniff. Sob. ". . . she was gone."

"Don't worry, dear." Miss Woodson pulled another tissue out of her pocket. "I'm sure she'll turn up."

Brittany howled. "No, she won't! I'll never find my Fifi."

"Darcy will," Sammy Lee said.

Everybody stared.

Brittany stopped sobbing. "What?"

"Darcy's a detective," Sammy said. "She'll find Fifi." He gave me the sort of smile you give somebody when you've got them in a fix they can't get out of. "Won't you, Darcy?"

"Well . . ." I said.

"Sure, she will," Mandy said. She believed in me because she's my best friend. "You'll do it, won't you, D.J.?"

Ordinarily, Darcy J. Doyle, Daring Detective, would jump at a chance to solve a big case. This was different. Here I was in front of Miss Woodson and the whole fifth grade, not to mention their parents and pets. "Well . . ."

"Perhaps we should call the police?" Miss Woodson suggested. It sounded like a good idea to me.

"The police?" Brittany turned pale at the

idea. "I . . . uh . . . already talked to the police. Naturally. First thing. They said . . . uh . . . that they only find missing persons . . . not missing dogs." She wiped her eyes with the remains of the tissue Miss Woodson had given her.

"You find missing dogs, don't you, Darcy?" Sammy asked.

"Well, sure, but . . ." I wasn't sure I wanted to find Brittany Barthwell's dog, Fifi.

"And you've got your faithful mutt, Max, right here to help you." Sammy patted Max lightly on top of the head.

I was insulted. "Max is no mutt," I said. "He's a trained attack animal." I grinned innocently. "Want a demonstration?"

Sammy looked as if he weren't quite sure if I were kidding or not. He pulled his hand away from Max's head and backed up. "Yeah," he said. "I want you to demonstrate how you solve these big cases you're always telling us about."

"She'd *never* be able to find Fifi!" Brittany sounded so positive, it made me mad. I'd treated her like a friend for two whole weeks now, and this was the thanks I got.

"It would be a piece of cake," I said, then regretted it the minute the words were out of my mouth.

"All right!" Sammy Lee thumped me on the back. The kids started clapping and cheering. The dogs and cats started yowling. And the parents looked as if they were really sorry they'd gotten involved in the pet show in the first place.

Brittany looked as if she'd eaten the Bayside Elementary cafeteria's famous noodle surprise. "But she *can't* look for Fifi." She blushed when everyone sort of stared at her. She even gave me a weak smile. "I mean ... I wouldn't want Darcy to go to all that trouble."

My Sunday school teacher was right. I *was*

surprised. This was the first time Brittany Barthwell had ever been worried about someone else. Maybe the Special Project wasn't such a silly idea after all.

I put a hand on Brittany's shoulder. "It wouldn't be any trouble," I said. I got carried away by the spirit of the moment. "I wouldn't even charge you my usual fee."

"But . . ." Brittany looked desperate. "The pet show. And our spelling quiz. And . . ."

Miss Woodson handed Brittany a fresh tissue. "The pet show and the spelling quiz can wait. Finding Fifi is more important." She gave me an encouraging smile. "If Darcy and Max are willing, I don't think it would do any harm to let them try."

CHAPTER 4

Miss Woodson had sent home most of the parents and all of the other pets, but we still had quite an audience. Miss Woodson, our teacher's aide, two volunteer parent chaperones, and twenty-six fifth graders marched through the front gate of Milton Park. The palm of my hand was sweaty as I held onto Max's leash.

"Why did you come through the park?" I asked Brittany Barthwell.

She looked about the way you'd look if you were about to take a big test you'd forgotten to study for. "It's a shortcut," she said. "From the house where Mom . . ." She stopped. "From my house." She pointed through the park toward Bayside Heights, one of the richest neighborhoods in town.

I nodded to Mandy, who had volunteered to be my assistant. "Write that down," I told her. Usually Daring Detectives like to take their own notes, but it was all I could do to hold on to Max. He kept pulling at his leash.

"Easy, Max," I said. "You'll get your chance." I smiled at Miss Woodson. "Good old Max," I told her. "Always anxious to get on the case."

She smiled back, but it was the sort of smile you'd give a little kid who had just told you all about Santa Claus. It made me more anxious than ever to crack the case.

"Couldn't somebody bring you to school today?" I asked Brittany. I was surprised she and her fancy show dog hadn't been delivered to the schoolyard by limousine.

"Uh . . ." She chewed at her lower lip. "The

chauffeur had to take Mother to a meeting at her club."

I was sorry I'd asked. Brittany's mother and father never came to any of the programs at school. She looked as if it really bothered her.

"Show me exactly where Fifi ran away," I said.

"Fifi did *not* run away!" she protested. "She chased a squirrel."

I sighed. Everything I said seemed to upset her. "Sorry," I said. I nodded to Mandy. "Write that down. *Chased a squirrel.*" Mandy scribbled away in my notebook. At least *she* looked as if she were having a wonderful time. "Show me where Fifi saw the squirrel."

Brittany led us to the crosswalk between the path to the old carousel and the path to the duck pond. "It was right here." She sniffled a few times and I wondered if Miss Woodson had remembered to bring more tissues.

"Hmmm." I studied the area. The place was full of paths, trees, bushes, and squirrels. There wasn't a poodle in sight. "Which way did they go?"

Brittany wasn't the world's best eyewitness. She hesitated, trying to make up her mind. Finally, she waggled a finger in the direction of the duck pond. "That way," she said.

I nodded to Mandy, who scribbled some more. "Well," I said. "Let's start there." I moved forward a couple of steps.

Brittany grabbed me by the arm. "I already looked there! I've looked *everywhere!* This is just a big waste of time."

"You would have been upset," I said. "Maybe you missed something. I think we should look again."

"Maybe Max should look for us," Sammy Lee said. It was a challenge, not a suggestion.

I glared at Sammy Lee. "Bloodhounds do not

look. They sniff," I said. "Too bad we don't have anything of Fifi's so he can catch the scent. He'd find her in no time."

"We have Brittany," Sammy pointed out. "Fifi's been all over you, hasn't she?" he asked her.

"Well . . . of course," she said. "But—"

"It can't hurt, Brittany," Miss Woodson interrupted. "You want to find Fifi. And we don't have much time." She glanced at her watch. "We have to be back for lunch in another hour."

"I guess it would be all right," Brittany said.

I dragged Max over. "Sniff, boy," I told him. He didn't need to be told twice. He jumped up, put his paws on Brittany's shoulders, and started licking her face.

"He's supposed to smell her, not wash her," Sammy Lee told me.

Everybody thought it was funny but me and Brittany. "Ugh!" She wiggled and shoved. "Get this slobbering beast off of me."

Max is no beast, and he only slobbers a little. I reminded myself that Brittany Barthwell was my Special Project and my client. "He seems to like you," I said. I couldn't understand why. I pulled Max down. "Hold out your hands so he can sniff them," I told Brittany. "Maybe he can catch the scent there."

She held her hands way out from her body and wrinkled up her nose as Max sniffed and licked her palms. I let her squirm for a minute, then pulled Max away again. Brittany wiped her hands on her dress. "Ugh," she said again.

I ignored her. Good old Max was pulling and straining at the leash. "He's on to something!" I said. "Get her, Max!" I ordered. "Go get Fifi!"

Max yelped twice, ran two circles around Brittany, then took off down the path that led to the duck pond. Twenty-six cheering fifth graders and four panting adults ran close behind.

CHAPTER 5

Nose in the air, ears flapping in the breeze, Max led us straight to the refreshment stand. The smell of hot, buttered popcorn filled the air.

"Some bloodhound!" Sammy Lee said.

Miss Woodson gave me the sort of look you'd give someone who just dumped his noodle surprise down the front of his shirt in the school cafeteria. "Perhaps Max is just hungry?" she suggested.

I didn't see how he could be since he'd already eaten a dozen cat-shaped sugar cookies Mrs. Rivera had sent in for the pet show. I thumped Max on the head. "Good old Max," I said. "You thought Fifi would head straight for the food stand, didn't you?" I made a big show of looking around. I shook my head. "Sorry, Max," I said. "Fifi isn't here."

Whining pitifully, Max pulled me toward the stand. Sammy Lee laughed loudly. "If we ever have missing popcorn, at least we'll know who to hire," he said.

Max pulled at his leash and whined some more. I was annoyed, but not at Max. "He's just anxious to interrogate a possible witness," I told Sammy.

When he isn't teasing somebody, Sammy doesn't have a lot to say. "Huh?"

"Someone who might have seen Fifi," I told Sammy. I shook my head at him as if he really should have figured it out for himself. I nodded to Mandy. "Be sure you take all this down." I let Max drag me over to the popcorn window. The whole fifth grade followed.

The girl smiled a big smile when she saw the crowd. "Popcorn for everybody?" she said.

"Not right now," I told her. Her smile disappeared. I introduced myself. "I'm Darcy J. Doyle, Daring Detective. I'm working on a big case."

She didn't seem too impressed. "I've got popcorn to make," she said. "And dogs aren't allowed to put their paws up on the counter like that."

"I only have a few questions," I told her. Mandy stood by with the notebook and pencil while I pulled Max down. "Have you seen a poodle go by here today?"

The popcorn girl was washing Max's paw prints from the countertop. "Sure," she said, as if it were a dumb question. "About nine-thirty."

I smiled. Now I was getting somewhere. "Fancy white poodle with pink toenails and ribbons?"

She shrugged. "Pink, red, yellow, blue. I didn't notice. The ribbons are always different, but the dog is always the same."

I didn't understand. "The same what?" I asked her.

She made a dumb-question face at me again. "The same dog," she said. "The same dog that goes by here every day a couple of times a day. In the morning and in the afternoon, about the time the kids come through from school."

I turned to Brittany. "Could that be your dog?" I asked.

It seemed to take her a while to decide. Finally, she shook her head. "We never bring Fifi to the park."

"Fifi!" the popcorn girl said. "That's the one." She squinted at Brittany. "Hey! You know the dog I mean. You asked me for a dish of water for her that day it was so hot. The day you were taking her picture."

We all looked at Brittany. "Oh!" she said, as if she'd forgotten all about it. "Mr. Windemere's dog! It looked so much like Fifi I asked him if I could take its picture." She laughed a strange kind of laugh. "Isn't it funny that they're both named Fifi?"

"Yeah," I said. "Funny." I nodded to Mandy, who scribbled it down in my notebook. Something was very funny, but I had no idea what it was.

Twenty-five fifth graders, four adults, and a popcorn girl looked at me, as if to say, "What now, Darcy J. Doyle, Daring Detective?" I sighed. This investigation was not going well. "Well, so much for that lead," I said.

"And so much for Darcy J. Doyle and her faithful bloodhound, Max," Sammy Lee said.

Miss Woodson stepped between us before I could slug him. She glanced at her watch. "We still have forty minutes. Perhaps we should divide into groups and search the park," she suggested. "Just in case Brittany's Fifi is still—"

She didn't get to finish. Max took off, pulling me along behind him like a kite at the end of a string. Good old Max. I knew he wouldn't let me down. Twenty-six fifth graders cheered and chanted as we followed him across the lawn and between the bushes. "Max! Max! Max!"

Around the duck pond, through the sandbox, under the monkey bars, behind the rest rooms, and over to a big clump of maple trees he ran. He stopped so suddenly, I nearly stepped on his tail. He sat there, ears perked up, tongue hanging out, nose pointed up the trunk of a tree. He had a silly, self-satisfied grin on his face.

Twenty-six panting fifth graders and four huffing adults looked up to see what he was staring at. I sort of hoped it would be Brittany Barthwell's dog, Fifi, but I knew it wasn't likely. Several people groaned. Sammy Lee chuckled loudly. Miss Woodson looked as if she couldn't quite make up her mind whether to laugh or cry.

I straightened my shoulders. "How about that!" I said proudly. "Good old Max has led us right to Fifi's squirrel."

CHAPTER 6

I was glad it was Saturday. I wouldn't have to face Miss Woodson, Sammy Lee, Brittany Barthwell, and the whole fifth grade for another two days. I pulled the covers up over my head.

My brother Allen came into my room without knocking. "It's ten o'clock. Mom wants to know if you're going to stay there all day."

"I'm going to stay here the rest of my life," I said.

The idea didn't worry Allen much. "Can I have your skateboard since you won't be using it?" he asked.

"Go away, Allen Doyle," I warned him.

I don't know if he was trying to make me feel better or rub it in. He said, "Just because the whole school knows about you and Max and how dumb you looked—"

I threw my pillow at him. I reached down and picked up a sneaker and threatened to throw that too. He ran out the door calling, "*Mom!*"

I dropped the sneaker, pulled my covers back over my head, and scrunched shut my eyes. It wasn't very comfortable lying there without a pillow, but I was too lazy and cross to get up and get it. I lay there feeling sorry for myself until something cold and wet and furry slipped under the cover and nudged me on the arm.

Max kissed me on the nose and whined his apologies. "It's not your fault," I told him. "I'm supposed to be the great detective." I scratched behind his ears. "And I still say it was the same squirrel."

"You'll never solve the case lying in bed."

I pulled down the covers and saw my father
standing in the doorway, a breakfast tray in his
hands. He came over and set it on my lap. It had
all my favorites. French toast with powdered
sugar. Crispy bacon. Orange juice. Max jumped
up in the bed beside me and started to drool
over my plate.

Dad didn't even yell at him to get down. "What's this for?" I asked him. "I'm not sick. It's not my birthday. And report cards aren't due for another two weeks." I took a big bite of the french toast. It was wonderful.

Dad grinned. "Consider it advance payment," he said.

I washed down the toast with a gulp of orange juice. "Advance payment for what?" I asked.

"For solving the Case of the Pampered Poodle," he told me. "Or at least giving it the best try you can."

I put down my fork. "I don't want to hear another word about that dumb dog!" I told him. "I already tried finding Fifi, and look what happened! Humiliated in front of the whole fifth grade! I'll never be able to show my face at school again."

Dad gave me the sort of eye-to-eye look that

makes you nervous even when you haven't done anything bad. "Maybe you'd get further if you stopped worrying about Max and Sammy Lee and what your classmates think and start going about it like a real detective," he said. He headed toward the door.

Dad was real big on always doing your best and finishing whatever you start. I had a feeling that was what he was getting at. "Do you really think I can find Fifi?" I asked him.

He stopped, his hand on the doorknob. "I don't know, Darcy." He winked at me. "But Sherlock Holmes would never give up this easily."

Leave it to Dad to throw Sherlock Holmes at somebody at a time like this. I couldn't let either of them down. And Brittany Barthwell *was* my Special Project. I knew how upset I'd be if Max had disappeared. I'd want somebody to try to find him, and I was supposed to be treating

Brittany the way I wanted to be treated myself, whether she deserved it or not. I handed Max a bite of French toast and dug into my breakfast.

Dad was right. Sherlock Holmes would never give up so easily. Just because my first try didn't work out very well, didn't mean I couldn't do it. After all, Daring Detectives run into all sorts of dead ends and obstacles when they're working on a big case. I started thinking of a bunch of people I could talk to, things I could do. "Want to give finding Fifi another try, Max?" I asked.

He stared at my bacon and drooled a little. "Woof! Woof!" he said.

Good old Max. Even Sherlock Holmes would have been proud.

CHAPTER 7

I recognized Brittany Barthwell's house the minute I saw it. She had shown us the picture more than once. Big iron gate. Long, curved driveway. White pillars on the front porch. Old stone house. Fifteen rooms and five bathrooms. All taken care of by a butler, a cook, a gardener, a chauffeur, and a live-in maid. Brittany had made sure to tell us all about them.

I pressed the buzzer at the gate. A gruff, bored-sounding voice came out of the box. "May I help you, Madam?"

I looked behind me to see if he was talking to somebody else.

"You. In the red sweater." Now the voice sounded gruff, bored, and impatient. "What do you want?"

I'd never had a conversation with a box before. I leaned over closer. "I'm Darcy J. Doyle, Daring Detective."

The voice coughed. "How nice," it said. "And just what can I do for you, Miss Doyle?"

Nobody ever called me Miss Doyle. I kind of liked it. I straightened my shoulders, trying to make myself look taller and older. "I'd like to see Brittany," I said.

"Brittany?" The voice sounded like he'd never heard of her.

"Brittany Barthwell," I said. "She's a . . ." I couldn't quite get out the word *friend*. "She's a classmate of mine."

"Oh." The voice sounded like Brittany had looked when she'd wrinkled up her nose at Max's picture. "You mean Millie's girl. She's

only here on weekdays, when Millie's working. You'll have to see her at home." There was a click and the box stopped sputtering.

I pressed the buzzer again. "I told you . . ." The voice sounded gruff, bored, impatient, *and* angry. "She's at home. Now run off like a good little girl."

"But—" The box clicked off again. I hated to do it, but Daring Detectives are stubborn. Besides, the "good little girl" part annoyed me. I pressed the buzzer a third time. "Please," I said, before the voice could yell at me. "I thought this *was* Brittany's home."

The voice laughed a short, gruff sort of laugh. It sounded sort of rusty, as if it didn't laugh very often. "Hardly." There was a pause. "If you promise to go away, I'll give you her address."

I promised. The box clicked off. A few minutes later it clicked on again. "2496 Wilmont," the voice told me. I wrote it in my notebook.

There were no big, fancy stone houses on Wilmont. I stopped in front of an old brick apartment building. The house number was painted on the front door in crooked black numerals. 2496.

I was really confused. "This can't be the right place," I muttered. I climbed the stairs, pushed open the front door, and peered at the row of mailboxes just inside the door. Henry. Rosetti. Yon. Barthwell. Miller. Washington. I pushed the button under the Barthwell mailbox.

A few seconds later a lady's voice answered. It sounded tired and out of breath. "Yes?"

I was getting used to talking to boxes. "I'm looking for Brittany Barthwell," I said. "I'm Darcy Doyle."

The voice sounded surprised and pleased. "Darcy! Brittany talks about you all the time! Come on up. Apartment B, third floor."

It was a long climb. A tall, thin woman in a

pair of faded jeans and a worn blue turtleneck sweater met me in the hallway. "I'm Brittany's mother, Millie Barthwell." She smiled warmly. "And you must be Darcy!" She held out her hand.

I remembered the pictures Brittany had shown us of her mother. A short, blonde woman wearing a fancy fur coat and dangly diamond earrings. This woman didn't look anything like her. I didn't feel confused any more, but I did feel sick, and sort of sorry for Brittany Barthwell. I took the hand her mother offered. "I'm a friend of your daughter's," I said.

CHAPTER 8

Sometimes Daring Detectives find out a little more than they really want to know. "We aren't allowed to have a dog in this small apartment," Mrs. Barthwell had told me. "So she plays with Mr. Windemere's dog every afternoon about this time."

I went home and picked up Max and walked him over to Milton Park to look for Brittany. I didn't know what I would say to her.

As we came around the corner of the carousel Max caught sight of another squirrel. He was off and running so fast he pulled the leash from

my hand, just the way Brittany said Fifi had done. Like the fancy house and the show ribbons, she'd made her lies all sound so real.

I chased him back around the carousel, through the bushes, and over the hill. I stopped to catch my breath, one hand on my side, the other over my eyes to shade out the sun. I saw a blur of brown fur heading toward the popcorn stand. Good old Max didn't know the case was solved. He was trying to pick up Fifi's trail again.

I ran down the hill, around the washrooms, and right into Brittany Barthwell. She was sitting on a bench with an elderly gentleman in a brown tweed suit. He had a green-bowed, fluffy white poodle in his arms.

Brittany had her own hands full. Max was practically sitting on top of her, his paws on her shoulders, his nose buried in the bag of popcorn she tried to hold up, over her head, in her left hand. "Get down, will you!" She pushed and shoved, but she couldn't budge him.

I ran over and pulled him away. Mushy popcorn kernels dribbled out of his mouth. "Max!" I grabbed his leash and held him back. It took some doing. "Leave Brittany and her popcorn alone!"

When I had Max more or less under control, Brittany introduced me to the gentleman. "This is Mr. Windemere. He's traveled all over the world."

She looked in my direction, and I wondered what she'd say about me. "And this is Darcy Doyle." She hesitated, giving me a funny sort of grin. "A much better detective than I thought."

Mr. Windemere scratched under Max's chin. "Every good detective needs a good dog," he said.

I smiled. "That's my faithful bloodhound, Max." Mr. Windemere didn't contradict me. I liked him a lot. Since he'd said something nice about my dog, I thought I should say something nice about his. I patted Fifi on the head. She wasn't so bad once you got to know her. She licked my hand, the way Max would do. "She must be smart to win all those ribbons," I said.

Mr. Windemere nodded proudly. "You'll have to come over some time and see them. Brittany can bring you and we'll have tea. Brittany and Fifi are the best of friends."

"I know. Brittany's told us all about her." I scratched the dog behind the ears. "Too bad you couldn't come to our pet show, Fifi," I said.

Brittany stared at me for a while before she said anything. "I was going to bring her," she said at last. "We had it all arranged. But Mr. Windemere's sister got sick. He had to go over to Westhaven on Thursday night and the pet show was Friday morning." She looked away, toward the popcorn stand. "I didn't want everybody laughing at me. So I said she was missing." Her face was pale, her eyes sad. "I didn't know what else to do."

I knew what it felt like to have everybody laugh at you. I sat down beside her on the bench. "I talked to your mother. She's real nice," I told her.

Brittany didn't seem all that surprised to hear that I'd met her. "Yeah," Brittany said. "She is." She chewed at her lower lip for a few seconds. "I guess you know she's the cook over at the Whitingtons."

I nodded. "She invited me over for lasagna."

Brittany smiled. "She makes a great lasagna."

We sat there for a while watching the dogs chase a pigeon. Brittany was the first one to talk, her voice so low and soft I could barely hear her. "I guess you'll have to tell everybody the truth. About Mom and Fifi . . . and me."

I thought about how smug and impossible Sammy Lee had been. I thought about the way everybody had laughed at me and Max. Somehow, it didn't bother me all that much any more. I knew that Darcy J. Doyle, Daring Detective, had solved the Case of the Pampered Poodle. And my faithful bloodhound, Max, had led me right to Fifi after all. I could write it all down in my notebook of Important Cases Solved by Darcy J. Doyle, Daring Detective. Dad and Sherlock Holmes would be satisfied. That's all that really mattered.

"It's your story," I told Brittany. "If you think they should know, you'll have to tell them yourself." I wasn't sure I could do it if I were in her place. Sooner or later, I thought she would.

I watched the two dogs playing together, big, furry Max and little, fluffy Fifi. They already acted like old friends. If it worked for them, it might work for me and Brittany. When she was just being herself … not trying to impress somebody … she was really sort of nice. Besides, we both liked dogs and lasagna. Who knew what else we might have in common?

"Our church youth group's having a skating party after prayer service tomorrow night," I told her. "We can bring a guest. Want to come?"

She smiled a bright, surprised smile, but it didn't last very long. "Why would you want *me* to come?" she wanted to know.

I could have told her that it was because she was my Special Project, but that wasn't the whole truth—not anymore. It felt a whole lot better to treat her the way I wanted to be treated because I *wanted* to, not because I *had* to. Maybe that was the surprise Mrs. Benson had been talking about all along

I smiled back at Brittany.

"Why not?" I said.